To Nelson, Vanessa, Ethan, Evelyn, Eliana, and Kai.
My very own very special children who inspired
this book...and inspire me every day!

-Love, Dad

www.mascotbooks.com

Elly Belly and the Can-Do Kids: The Winter Clothing Drive

For more information, please contact:
Mascot Books
620 Herndon Parkway, Suite 320
Herndon, VA 20170
info@mascotbooks.com

Library of Congress Control Number: 2020911905

CPSIA Code: PRT0121A
ISBN-13: 978-1-64543-423-8

Printed in the United States

Elly Belly
and the
CAN-DO KIDS
THE WINTER CLOTHING DRIVE

Ed Davies
Illustrated by
Stacy Hummel

Elly Belly was on her way to the Can-Do Kids Clubhouse. Today was community service day, and she could not wait to pick a project with her friends.

On her way to the clubhouse, she wondered how the Can-Do Kids would help their community this time.

Elly Belly saw a puppy shivering under a tree. She had an idea!

At the Can-Do Kids Clubhouse, Elly Belly told the others her plan. "Winter is here and it is cold outside. But some people don't have hats, gloves, or even coats. Let's collect winter clothing for the community!"

"Great idea!"
they all agreed.

Hats.

Gloves.

Sweaters, scarves, and...

At the park, the Can-Do Kids set up for the community clothing drive.

"I have a joke for you," said Silly Billy.

"Why did the snowman get all dressed up?"

"I don't know," Elly Belly replied.

"To go to the snow ball!" said Silly Billy.

Elly Belly laughed.

Suddenly, a large gust of wind blew and scattered the clothes all over the park.

"Don't worry Elly Belly," said Loosey Goosey. "We're the Can-Do Kids!"

"We can do it!"

Everyone had a special talent to contribute, and together, they could do anything!

Roll.

Stack.

Thumpa-thumpa-thump!

Bumpa-bumpa-bump!

The Can-Do Kids handed out winter clothes all afternoon. The hot chocolate helped keep everyone warm, too!

"Good work, team!" said Elly Belly.

She was so happy that her friends had helped the community get what they needed to stay warm all winter long.

"No matter how different we look or sound, we all share the same space," said Elly Belly. "And we each have special talents, to make the world a better place."

The Can-Do Kids Club: A special club where special kids with special talents do special things . . .

. . . to make the world a better place.